Foods From Friends and Neighbors

Acknowledgments
Executive Editor: Diane Sharpe
Supervising Editor: Stephanie Muller
Design Manager: Sharon Golden
Page Design: Simon Balley Design Associates
Photography: Eye Ubiquitous: page 13; Robert Harding: pages 10, 21; Image Bank: cover (top, middle), pages 19, 21 (inset), 25 (inset); Alex Ramsay: pages 15 (inset), 23, 25 ; Tony Stone: cover (bottom), pages 6-7, 9, 27; Zefa: page 15.

ISBN 0-8114-3802-3

Copyright © 1995 Steck-Vaughn Company.

All rights reserved. No part of the material protected by this copyright may be reproduced or utilized in any form or by any means, electronic or mechanical, including photocopying, recording, or by any information storage and retrieval system, without permission in writing from the copyright owner. Requests for permission to make copies of any part of the work should be mailed to: Copyright Permissions, Steck-Vaughn Company, P.O. Box 26015, Austin, TX 78755.
Printed in the United States of America.
British edition Copyright © 1994 Evans Brothers.

1 2 3 4 5 6 7 8 9 00 PO 00 99 98 97 96 95 94

Foods From Friends and Neighbors

Paul Humphrey

Illustrated by
Kareen Taylerson

Steck-Vaughn Company

"Mom, may I have another cookie?"

4

No, you shouldn't eat too many cookies.

Cookies and other sweets have too much sugar and fat. It is not good to eat too many sweets.

5

Which foods are good for us?

If you help me make dinner, I'll show you.

If you want to be healthy, it is important to eat the right kinds of food. This is called a balanced diet.

7

8

Foods with carbohydrates are very good for you. They give you energy.

9

Your body also needs protein. This is found in foods such as fish, meat, and nuts. Protein helps to build strong muscles.

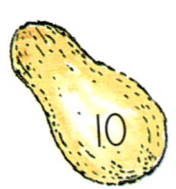

Sometimes we have meat for dinner.

Sometimes we have fish for lunch.

"I know it's important to eat fruits and vegetables."

"Yes, they have many vitamins."

Vitamins help your body work well.
They keep you feeling healthy.

13

Is all the food we eat grown nearby?

No, most of the food we eat comes from all over North America.

Some food is grown here, but much of it comes from other places. It is brought to our stores by trucks, trains, ships, or even planes.

"This box of noodles came from New Jersey."

"Why don't you look at some more boxes and cans?"

Labels on boxes and cans tell where the food came from.

"This flour came from Minnesota."

"That's the flour Mom used to make this bread!"

Wheat is grown in many places. It is harvested in late summer. Then the wheat usually is ground into flour.

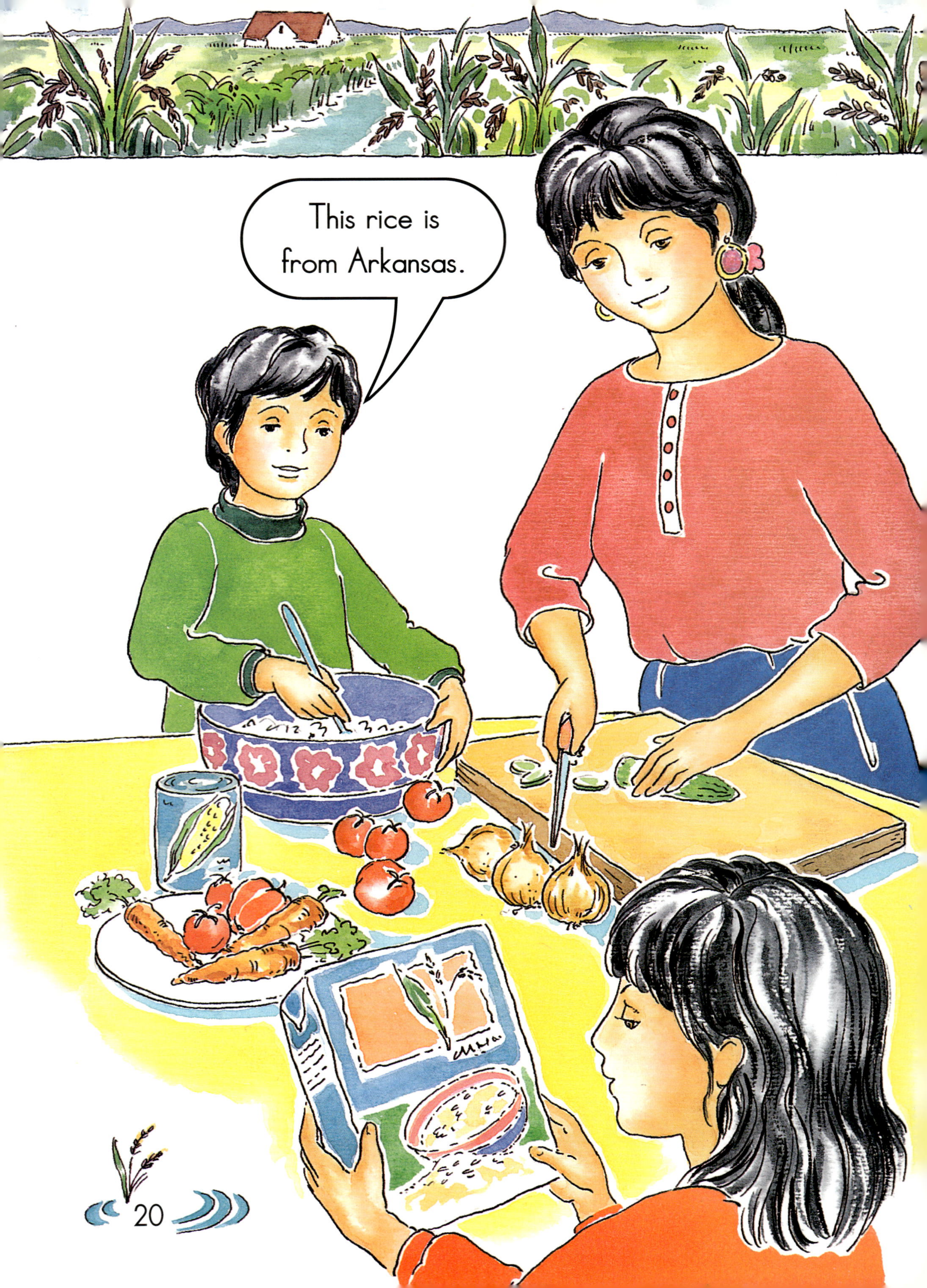
This rice is from Arkansas.

Rice is grown in places where it is warm and wet. There are more than 14,000 different kinds of rice.

This milk is from our town!

22

Milk can turn sour very quickly. So most stores get milk from a farm that is nearby.

Some milk is made into butter, cheese, and yogurt. These foods are called dairy products.

This canned fish came from Canada.
That will really taste good.

Canned and frozen fish come from different areas all over North America.

25

"These oranges came from Mexico."

"The pineapple came from Hawaii."

There are many kinds of fruits and vegetables. In the summer, some of them can be grown near your home. In the winter, they may need to be shipped from other places.

28

"Did you know that our dinner came from all over North America?"

There are many different kinds of food. It is important to eat a good balanced diet so you can stay healthy and fit.

Do you remember where these foods came from? The answers are on the last page, but don't look until you have tried to name each place.

1.

2.

3.

Index

Arkansas **20**

Balanced diet **6-7, 29**
Bread **8, 18**

Canada **24**
Carbohydrates **8-9**
Cereal **8**
Cookies **4-5**

Dairy products **23**

Energy **9**

Fish **10-11, 24-25, 30**
Flour **18-19**
Fruit **12-13, 27**

Hawaii **26**

Meat **10-11**
Mexico **26**
Milk **22-23**
Minnesota **18**
Muscles **10**

New Jersey **16**
Noodles **16, 30**
North America **14, 25, 29**
Nuts **10**

Oranges **26, 31**

Pineapple **26, 30**
Potatoes **8**
Protein **10**

Rice **20-21, 31**

Vegetables **12, 27**
Vitamins **12-13**

Wheat **19**

Answers: 1. New Jersey 2. Canada 3. Hawaii 4. Mexico 5. Arkansas

32